JUDY MOODY AND FRIENDS

Mrs. Moody
in The Birthday Jinx

Megan McDonald

illustrated by Erwin Madrid

based on the characters
created by Peter H. Reynolds

CANDLEWICK PRESS

For Janet Varney

M. M.

For my mom, Felicitas Madrid

E. M.

Text copyright © 2016 by Megan McDonald
Illustrations copyright © 2016 by Peter H. Reynolds
Judy Moody font copyright © 2003 by Peter H. Reynolds

Judy Moody®. Judy Moody is a registered trademark of Candlewick Press, Inc.

First edition 2016

Library of Congress Catalog Card Number 2015933256
ISBN 978-0-7636-8198-2 (hardcover)
ISBN 978-0-7636-8199-9 (paperback)

16 17 18 19 20 21 CCP 10 9 8 7 6 5 4 3 2 1

Printed in Shenzhen, Guangdong, China

MIX
Paper from
responsible sources
FSC® C008047
FSC
www.fsc.org

This book was typeset in ITC Stone Informal.
The illustrations were created digitally.

Candlewick Press
99 Dover Street
Somerville, Massachusetts 02144

visit us at www.candlewick.com

CONTENTS

CHAPTER 1

The Boss of Birthday 1

CHAPTER 2

The Mitten State 23

CHAPTER 3

Mummy Time 43

CHAPTER 1
The Boss of Birthday

Every year on Mom's birthday, something went wrong-not-right. Judy called it the Birthday Jinx.

But this year was going to be different. This year, Judy would be the boss of birthday. And this year, Stink was *not* going to get carsick. And this year, Dad would finally bake Mom's favorite—carrot cake.

She, Judy Moody, would break the Birthday Jinx once and for all.

"Hey, Stinkerbell," Judy said to her brother, "tomorrow is Mom's birthday. No getting sick this year. And you have to make her a really good present."

Stink looked up from building the
United Nations Headquarters out of
Snappos. "I have to *make* a present?"
he asked.

"You can't buy her a pack of gum like last year."

"What's wrong with gum? Mom likes gum."

"A handmade present says, *I love you* and *I care*. Gum does not say, *I love you*. Gum does not say, *I care*."

"What does gum say?"

"Gum says, *I only had a dollar*."

"I say talking gum is a pretty good present!" said Stink.

He looked at his Snappos. "Wait! I have an idea!"

"And Mom's present can't be made of Snappos," Judy said.

"Rats!" said Stink.

Next Judy went to her dad. "I'm the boss of Mom's birthday this year," she told him. "This year, Mom's cake has to be carrot cake."

"Do I have to make it myself?"

"From scratch," said Judy. "Cake made from scratch says, *I love you* and *I care*."

"Hmm," said Dad. "I say a talking cake is a pretty good present!"

Finally, Judy got started on her own gift for Mom. She tried making earrings out of seashells, but she ended up with a pair of glue globs.

She tried making a Popsicle-stick picture frame, but couldn't eat enough Popsicles.

Judy even tried to draw a picture of a hug, but it came out looking like a monkey.

Judy eyed her jar of
Make-a-Word beads.
All she had left were
X's, *Z*'s, and numbers.
Mom liked beads.
Mom liked bracelets.
Mom liked numbers;
she was always talking
up math. *Eureka!* The perfect idea.
A phone-number bracelet!

A phone-number bracelet was
better than glue-glob earrings. Better
than a Popsicle-stick picture frame.
Better than a drawing of a hug. A
phone-number bracelet would help
break the Birthday Jinx for sure.

That night, Judy could hardly sleep.
At last it was Mom's birthday.

Judy and Stink ran into Mom and Dad's room and bounced on the bed. "Happy birthday, Mom!"

Mom pulled the covers up over her head.

"Kids," said Dad. "We should let Mom sleep in on her birthday."

"Who can sleep when there are presents to open?" Judy said.

Mom sat up and rubbed her eyes. "I'm awake now."

"Open my present first," said Judy. She handed Mom a small box tied with rainbow yarn.

Judy could not wait to see Mom's face light up like a birthday candle! Mom tore off the wrapping. Mom lifted the lid.

Mom's face *didn't* light up like a birthday candle.

"A bracelet," said Mom, "with numbers."

"Not just *any* numbers," said Judy. "Our phone number."

"Sorry, wrong number!" said Stink. "That's not even our phone number."

"I ran out of sevens," Judy explained. "Just pretend the fives are sevens, Mom, and you'll never forget our phone number."

"Except she will forget, because that's not—"

"Stink," Dad warned.

Stink was right. The fives-not-sevens phone-number bracelet was a bad idea. It was the Birthday Jinx all over again.

Judy ran to her room and came back with her Six-Year Pen. "You can have this instead," she told Mom. "It still has four years left in it. I promise."

"Open mine next," Stink urged. Mom untied the shoelace ribbon. She tore off the Sunday comics.

Inside was a rock. A painted rock
with googly eyes.

"You got Mom a rock?" Judy asked.

"It's a pet rock *and* a paperweight,"
said Stink.

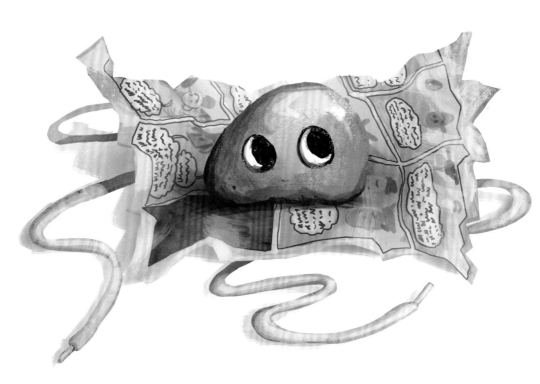

"Oh, look," said Mom. "It even says
MOM on the bottom."

"I made it by hand," Stink told her.
"That says, *I care.*"

"A rock does not say I care," Judy
muttered. "Here, Mom. Open Dad's
gift."

Whatever Dad got, it *had* to break
the Birthday Jinx.

Mom tore off the wrapping paper.

"Oh!" Mom looked surprised. "A . . . glue gun. Or is it a cake decorator?"

"It's a label maker," said Dad.

"Not just *any* label maker," said Judy, reading the box. "The Dynamo Office Buddy 2000 Embosser."

"Now you can label the kids' backpacks and lunch boxes and all sorts of things," said Dad.

SHELF OF HONOR

"You can label my present so everybody knows it's not just a rock," said Stink.

"And you can make a label that says SHELF OF HONOR where you can keep all your presents," Judy said, beaming at her father.

"Can you tell we care?" asked Stink.

"You're not supposed to *say* it, Stink," said Judy. "The present is supposed to say it for you."

"But I want to make sure Mom can hear what the presents are saying."

"I can hear," said Mom with a wide smile. "Loud and clear."

CHAPTER 2
The Mitten State

"Let's go do something way-not-boring for Mom's birthday," Judy said after breakfast.

"I call Reptile Mania," said Stink.

"I call glow-in-the-dark bowling," said Judy.

"I call we let Mom choose," said Dad. "It is her day."

"I choose . . . a nature walk," said Mom. "I hear that snowy owls have been spotted at Smugglers' Bay."

By the time the Moodys piled into the car, it was almost lunchtime. "Let's stop to eat first," said Dad.

"I call Mac and Cheesy!" said Stink.

"I call the Bowling Alley Diner," said Judy.

"I call we let Mom choose," said
Dad.

"I love sushi," said Mom.

Judy tried not to make a face.
"Dead fish?"

Stink pinched his nose shut. "Sushi
is P.U."

The Moodys ended up at the Grilled Cheese Kitchen.

After lunch at the no-sushi Grilled Cheese Kitchen, they piled back into the car and headed to Smugglers' Bay.

Suddenly, Stink got an *uh-oh* look on his face.

"Not again! Are you sick or something?" Judy asked.

"Or something."

"Oh, no. The Birthday Jinx is back!"

Mom felt Stink's forehead. "You don't feel warm," said Mom.

"I, um, forgot to tell you about some homework. I have to dress up as a United State."

Mom blinked super fast.

"And I need my costume by tomorrow."

"Stink!" Dad said. "It's Mom's birthday."

"Dressing up as a state is a big second-grade deal," Judy told Stink. "Do you know how long it took me to become South Dakota?"

"How long?" Stink asked.

"Long," said Judy.

Mom took a deep breath. "We can grab some supplies at a crafts store, then head home and work on the costume."

"What about your nature walk?" Judy asked.

"I can walk around the backyard later," said Mom.

"The backyard doesn't have snowy owls," said Judy.

"It has sparrows," said Stink hopefully.

Judy gave Stink the hairy eyeball.

Mom turned to Stink. "So, what state do you have to be?"

"Michigan. The Mitten State. Michigan is shaped like a giant mitten."

"Then a giant mitten you shall be!" Mom said.

As soon as they got home, Mom helped Stink cut two Stink-size mitten shapes out of blue foam. She cut a round hole in one mitten for Stink's face.

While Dad was busy baking not-from-a-box carrot cake in the kitchen, Mom set up her sewing machine. She zipped up one side of Michigan and zoomed down the other. She snipped and sewed all afternoon.

At last, Mom slipped the state of Michigan over Stink's head. Stink spun around the room. "Look at me! I'm the Lower Peninsula!"

"You look like a giant left-handed mitten," said Judy.

"I'm smitten with this mitten," said Mom, tugging the costume here and there.

"Thanks, Mom!" said Stink. "Um, I was thinking . . . can you make a robin, too? That's the state bird. And maybe a flag? Apple blossom is the state flower—"

Mom slumped in her chair, a tape measure draped around her neck. "I'm pooped."

"Hel-lo?" said Judy. "It's Mom's birthday, Stink. She needs Mom time."

So Stink drew pictures of robins and apple blossoms and brook trout and even a mastodon, the state fossil. Judy helped cut out the shapes and glue them to the mitten.

"Is that everything?" Mom asked after Stink glued on a sequin for Lansing, the state capital.

Stink checked his homework sheet to make double-sure he hadn't forgotten anything. In less than a Detroit minute, his face went as white as a marshmallow.

The Michigan mitten crumpled at the knees and sank to the floor like the wreck of that ship, the *Edmund Fitzgerald.* Kal-a-ma-zoo!

"Hey, Michigan," said Judy, poking Stink in the state capital. "What's wrong?"

39

"I messed up," he moaned. "It's a major, mastodon-size mess up."

"What do you mean?" asked Mom.

"I'm not even supposed to be Michigan," Stink moaned.

"What are you supposed to be?" asked Judy.

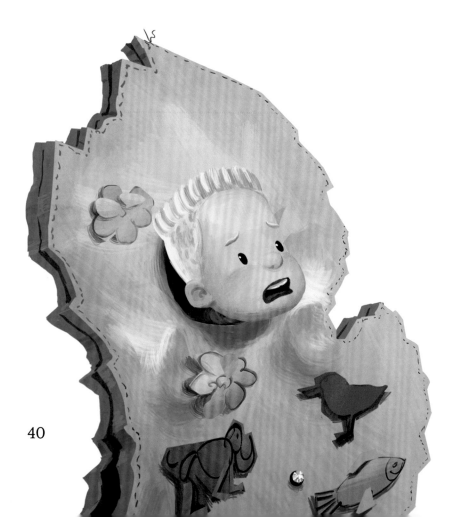

"Min-min-min," Stink stammered.
He could hardly get the word out.
"Minnesota!" he wailed.

CHAPTER 3
Mummy Time

"It's that Birthday Jinx again!" said
Judy. "Mom, *I'll* help Stink change
Michigan to Minnesota. We'll just add
a bunch of lakes or something."

"Ten thousand lakes," said Stink.
"Minnesota is the Land of Ten
Thousand Lakes."

"That's a lot of lakes," said Judy.

"Officially there are eleven thousand eight hundred and forty-two lakes, but I think we can get away with only making ten thousand."

"Yikes. We better hurry up and start. Mom, do you want to take your nature walk in the backyard now?"

"Right now I want to take a nap. I'm going to close my eyes for fifteen minutes."

Mom curled up on the couch. Judy brought her a fluffy pillow. Stink covered her up with his cozy sleeping bag. Soon Mom was snoozing peacefully.

Judy cut out a picture of a muffin from a cooking magazine. "Here, take off the Michigan stuff and glue this on," she told Stink. "Blueberry is the Minnesota state muffin."

"I bet the state weather is snow," said Stink. "I know how to make a paper snowflake."

"There's no such thing as state—"

Chirr-up! Chirr-up! Mom rolled onto her side. *Chirr-up! Chirr-up!* Mom rolled onto her back. *Chirr-up! Chirr-up!* Mom woke up. "Sounds like there's a cricket in the house," she said, and rolled onto her other side.

Ribbet! Ribbet! "Now I hear frogs!" Mom said, sitting up. "Does anybody else hear frogs?"

"It's my musical sleeping bag," Stink told her. "It makes nature sounds to help you get sleepy."

"How do I turn the sounds off?" Mom asked.

"It only makes noise when you move," said Stink, "so make like a mummy and you'll be fine."

Mom/Mummy lay back down and drifted off to sleep again.

"Acorn Lake, Alice, Artichoke, Bald Eagle Lake . . . ," Judy murmured.

Click-click, click-click, click-click-click.

"Are the crickets back?" Mom asked, opening her eyes. "Why do I feel like I'm counting lakes in my sleep?"

"Oops, sorry," said Judy. "We're using your Dynamo Office Buddy 2000 to label the lakes in Minnesota."

"Dynamo," said Mom. She pulled the sleeping bag up over her ears.

Chirr-up. Chirr-up. Ribbet.

"Big McDonald, Big Rice, Button
Box . . . " Stink mumbled as he glued.

Click-click-click.

EEE-EEE-EEE! EEE-EEE-EEE!

Mom bolted upright. "Fire! Call
nine-one-one!"

EEE-EEE-EEE!

All at once, the screeching stopped. Dad came hurrying out of the kitchen. "A million sorries. I was baking your cake and set off the smoke alarm," he said. "How was your nap?"

"Eventful," said Mom. "I think I've had enough nap for one day."

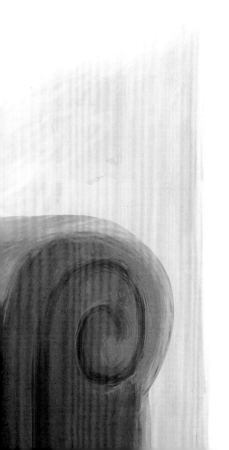

A half hour later, Dad called, "Carrot-cake time!" Everybody crowded around the dining-room table and stared.

"Holy guacamole!" said Judy.

"Why is it . . . pukey green?" Stink asked.

"Avocado," said Dad. "I mashed some into the icing. I thought it would go well with the carrots."

Judy gulped. Stink gagged.

Dad turned out the lights and lit the candles.

"Make a wish!" Judy called.

Mom squeezed her eyes shut. Mom made a wish. Mom blew out the candles.

Dad cut the cake. The inside of the cake did not look very carroty.

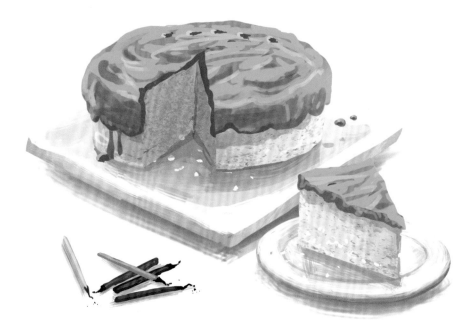

"Um, Dad, why is the carrot cake *white*?" Judy couldn't help asking.

"I thought it was strange, too," said Dad. "When I took the carrots out of the fridge, they seemed awfully pale to me."

Mom started to laugh.

"What's so funny?" asked Dad.

"Those weren't carrots," said Mom. "We're all out of carrots. Those were parsnips."

Dad's face went as white as the cake. "I made you *parsnip* cake?"

It was no use. Mom's birthday *was* jinxed. Judy scribbled out an IOU and handed it to her mother. "Mom, we owe you one un-jinxed birthday. Can we do over Mom's birthday tomorrow, Dad?"

"Please, no!" said Mom. "I mean—one birthday is enough to last me a whole year."

"I bet I know what you wished when you blew out the candles," said Judy. "I bet you wished that your birthday was not jinxed."

"My birthday was not jinxed," said Mom.

"But you didn't get to eat dead fish like you wanted," said Stink.

"No, but I did get to eat all my vegetables for the day in one slice of birthday cake."

"And you didn't get to go on a nature walk or see a snowy owl," said Judy.

"I didn't need to," said Mom. "I had a cricket-and-frog symphony in my very own living room."

"You couldn't even take a nap with all the noise," said Judy.

"Noise is the sound of family," said Mom. "And the best birthdays are full of noise."

Judy, Stink, Mom, and Dad piled onto the couch in one big snuggle.

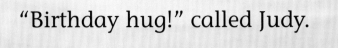

"Birthday hug!" called Judy.

And the hug did not look one bit like a monkey.

Mom wrapped the sleeping bag around them.

Chirr-up! Chirr-up! Ribbet!